Atul's Wonderful Christi

GW00809079

Written by Henley Santa
Introduction by Michael Rosen
Illustrations by Mudassir Abid

Introduction

One of the best ways you can help your children learn and learn to read is to share books with them.

- They get to know the sounds, rhythms and words used in the way we write. This is different from how we talk, so hearing stories helps children learn how to read.
- They think about the feelings of the characters in the book. This helps them as they go about their own lives with other people.
- They think about the ideas in the book. This helps them to understand the world.
- Sharing books and listening to what your children say about them shows your children that you care about what they think and who they are.

Michael Rosen
Writer and Poet
Children's Laureate (2007–9)

Thank you, Michael, for letting me share your introduction with my readers.

As far back as Atul could remember, he had wanted a dog.

He asked his mum every year and she always said, "We'll see."

At last, mum said, "Santa will bring you a dog this Christmas."

Just before Christmas came around there was a great flood and the river burst its banks.

The dog that Santa was going to give Atul was washed away in the flood. Santa was not able to find another dog for Atul anywhere.

Santa said to Atul's mum,

"All I have on my sleigh to give Atul is this drumstick. I will load it with Christmas magic, and we will see what happens."

"I must give him a present because he is such a good and kind boy."

"As soon as I finish my last few deliveries, I will look for his missing dog."

Atul was sad at first, but he made the best of it and treated the stick as if it was a dog.

"Look mum! I trained my stick to do tricks – he can do stay, lie down, play dead, roll over and fetch."

Mum laughed and called, "Atul take your stick and play outside."

Atul tied a bit of string round his stick and took it for a walk.

Across the river he met the village baker. She was surrounded by black smoke, coughing and crying.

"What's wrong?"

"The river flooded, and all my kindling is wet. I can't light my fire to bake my bread."

"I have my stick. It is dry and will burn well - you can break it up to start your fire."

Atul waited with the baker as she broke the stick and lit her fire. She started to bake the bread.

She was very grateful and gave Atul some flat bread called roti all spread with butter.

Atul thought, "What a strange Christmas. I wanted a dog, but I got a stick that turned into some bread."

Atul walked along. He heard a baby crying. The baby sounded very upset.

He saw the village potter, holding her baby, rocking him back and forth.

Atul said, "What is wrong with the baby?"

"My baby is really hungry, but the baker isn't baking because of the flood. So, we have no fresh bread for him."

Atul said, "I have this fresh, warm bread. You can have it for the baby."

The potter gave some of the roti to the baby. The baby stopped crying at last and fell asleep.

"Oh, thank you." said the grateful potter. "Here, Atul, have one of my big wash pots."

Atul said, "Thank you." and walked on.

He thought, "What a strange Christmas. I wanted a dog, but I got a stick that turned into some bread that turned into a pot."

Just then Atul heard someone shouting.

He crossed back over the river and saw the village laundry man shouting and kicking a broken wash pot.

Atul asked "What's wrong?"

The laundry man said, "I left my wash pot near the river last night. The flood has smashed it on the rocks and broken it. I can't do the laundry."

Atul said, "I have this big wash pot. You can have it."

The laundry man said that would be marvellous and thanked Atul.

Then he said, "Atul I have this coat that nobody has collected. You must have it."

He gave Atul a warm coat.

Atul thought to himself, "What a strange Christmas. I wanted a dog, but I got a stick that turned into some bread that turned into a pot that turned into a coat."

Atul walked on further and he saw an old man who was standing in wet underwear. The rest of his clothes were spread out on a bush to dry. He was shivering and quivering and sneezing.

"What happened?" asked Atul.

The man said, "I jumped into the river to rescue this little dog. He was caught on a tree branch in the water. My clothes are soaked through and I'm freezing."

Atul said, "I have this lovely coat. You can have it to get warm."

The man wrapped the coat around himself and gradually warmed up and stopped shivering.

The man said, "Thank you, Atul. Will you take this dog I rescued and give him a good home?"

Atul said, "Yes please. I always wanted a dog."

Atul went straight home with his dog, ready to surprise Mum.

He thought to himself, "What a strange and wonderful Christmas. I wanted a dog, but I got a stick that turned into some bread that turned into a pot that turned into a coat that turned into my very own dog."

"I will teach my dog good tricks."

For Eden, Ezra and Eliza
and the thousands of children who have
visited me over the last thirty-five years.

Thank you to my sons who helped
develop the story and to the team of
readers who helped to improve the book.

I hope you enjoyed "Atul's Wonderful Christmas".

However you felt about this book, would you please leave me a review on Amazon.

 For updates on this and future books and offers, please drop me an email on mike.facherty@tiscali.co.uk

If you enjoyed "Atul's Wonderful Christmas", I think you will love my other books "Santa and the Gingerbread Man" and "Santa and the Lighthouse".

Thank you.

Henley Santa

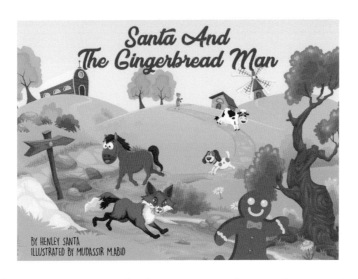

My first book, "Santa and the Gingerbread Man", is ideal for grown-ups to read aloud with young children and for older children to read themselves. It includes activities to entertain and help develop them at Christmas or any time of year. You can watch a video animation of it on YouTube at https://youtu.be/VclLmY7WiOg

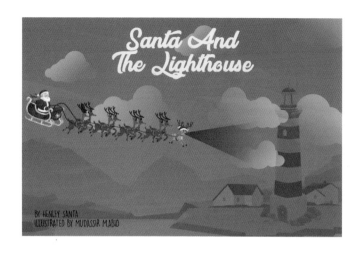

Even the glow from Rudolph's red nose can't help Santa Claus find the lighthouse on this foggy Christmas Night.

If they can't find it, the lighthouse keeper won't get his present.

But there is a greater risk than that. Ships at sea are in grave peril.

Can Santa Claus and his reindeer save the lighthouse keeper's Christmas and keep the crews on the ships safe?

Printed in Great Britain
by Amazon

49326957R00020